MOON JUMP

Mustapha Matura
Pictures by Jane Gifford

ALFRED A. KNOPF · NEW YORK

For Cayal and Maya,
Katherine and Rachael

This is a Borzoi Book published by Alfred A. Knopf, Inc.

Text copyright © 1988 by Mustapha Matura. Illustrations copyright © 1988 by Jane Gifford.
All rights reserved under International and Pan-American Copyright Conventions. Published
in the United States by Alfred A. Knopf, Inc., New York. Distributed by Random House,
Inc., New York. Originally published in Great Britain by William Heinemann Ltd., London.
First American Edition.

Manufactured in Hong Kong   1   2   3   4   5   6   7   8   9   10

Library of Congress Cataloging-in-Publication Data
Matura, Mustapha. Moon Jump.
Summary: A boy who loves to jump jumps all the way to the moon one night, where he meets
a moon man who also loves to jump.   [1. Jumping—Fiction. 2. Moon—Fiction]
I. Gifford, Jane, ill. II. Title.   PZ7.M4364Mo   1988   [E]   88-6788
ISBN 0-394-81976-4   ISBN 0-394-91976-9 (lib. bdg.)

Cayal loved to jump.

When he woke up in the morning,
he jumped out of bed,

then he jumped into the bath,

then he jumped into his pants,

then he jumped into his shoes.

He jumped from the chair to the floor

and from the floor to the sofa.

On the way to school he jumped in the park,

and when he got to school, he jumped
in the playground .

But best of all, he loved to jump when his daddy took him upstairs to put on his pajamas.

Then he would jump, jump, jump on his
mommy and daddy's bed.

One night Cayal began to jump higher,

and higher, and higher, until . . .

. . . with one enormous leap

he jumped all the way to the moon.

When he landed, he met a moon man.

"How did you get here?" the moon man asked.
"I jumped," said Cayal.

"I like jumping too," said the moon man.
"Shall we jump together?"

"Yes, please," said Cayal,
and they jumped and jumped
all over the moon.

Then the moon man said,
"Why don't we jump over to my house?"

"We can have cocoa and cake and
strawberries and cream."

"Oh yes, please," said Cayal,
and they jumped all the way over to
the moon man's house

and had cocoa and cake and
strawberries and cream.

Cayal said, "I feel sleepy."

"It's time to jump home then,"
said the moon man.

Cayal waved good-bye

and jumped really hard.

He jumped so hard that the
next thing he knew, he was landing
on his mommy and daddy's bed.

His daddy said, "Oh, there you are!"
and gave him a great big hug and
tucked him into his own bed.

Cayal stopped jumping and fell fast asleep.
Good night, Cayal.